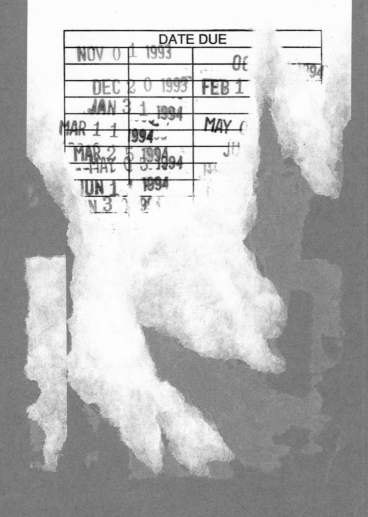

Grégoire Solotareff

THE OGRE AND THE FROG KING

GREENWILLOW BOOKS, NEW YORK

Once upon a time there was an ogre.

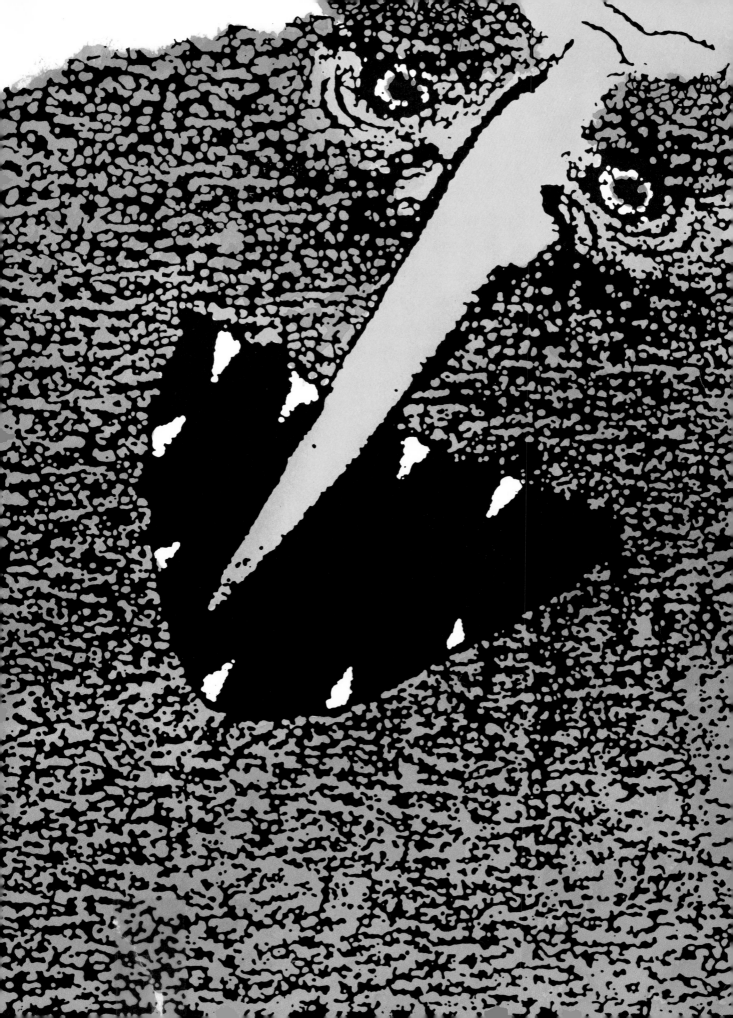

He lived in a big house

in the middle of the forest.

There was nothing he liked better than to sleep and eat, and he found little animals the tastiest of all.

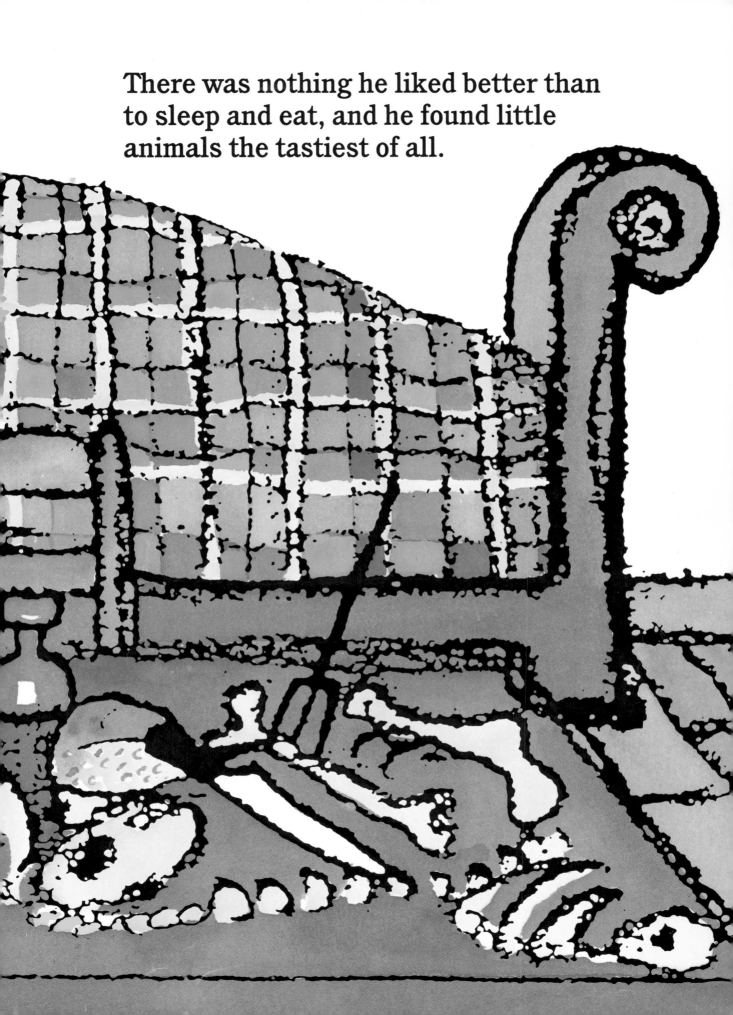

Sometimes he would go out at night

and hunt for supper by the light of the moon.

One day while the ogre was sleeping, a small frog, wearing a crown, jumped through the window.

He landed on the ogre's nose.

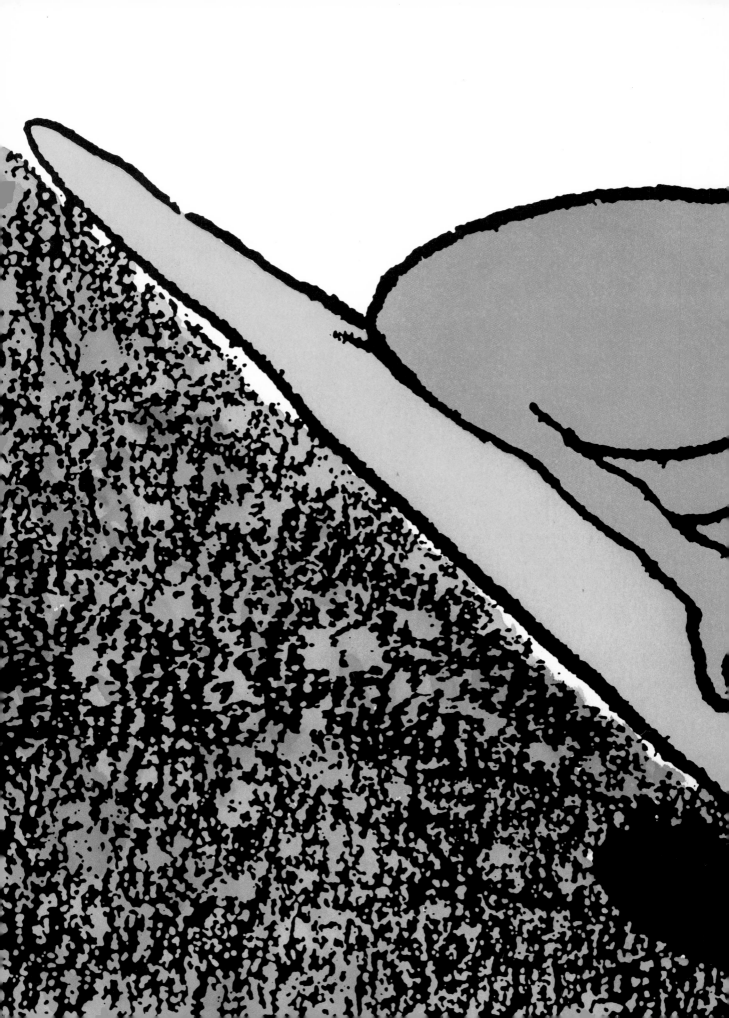

The ogre woke
with a start.
The frog looked
enormous.

The ogre was so frightened he hid
under the table.

The frog realized that he had the ogre at his mercy.

"I am the king of the frog giants," he said. "If you don't stop eating my friends, I will eat you."

"I promise," said the ogre.

He was too frightened to look up at the frog and see how small he really was.

"You must not leave the house," said the frog, "except to gather mushrooms. If I learn that you have eaten even the smallest field mouse, I will return and eat you."

The next day the ogre went out
to gather mushrooms.
On the way he met the frog.
"Hello, little frog," he said.
"Are you lost?"
The frog laughed to himself.
The ogre didn't recognize him.
"No, I'm not lost," he replied.
"But where are you going with
that knife and fork?"

"I am gathering mushrooms for my
   supper," said the ogre.
"I thought you only ate animals,"
   said the frog.
"Not anymore," said the ogre.
   And he walked away.

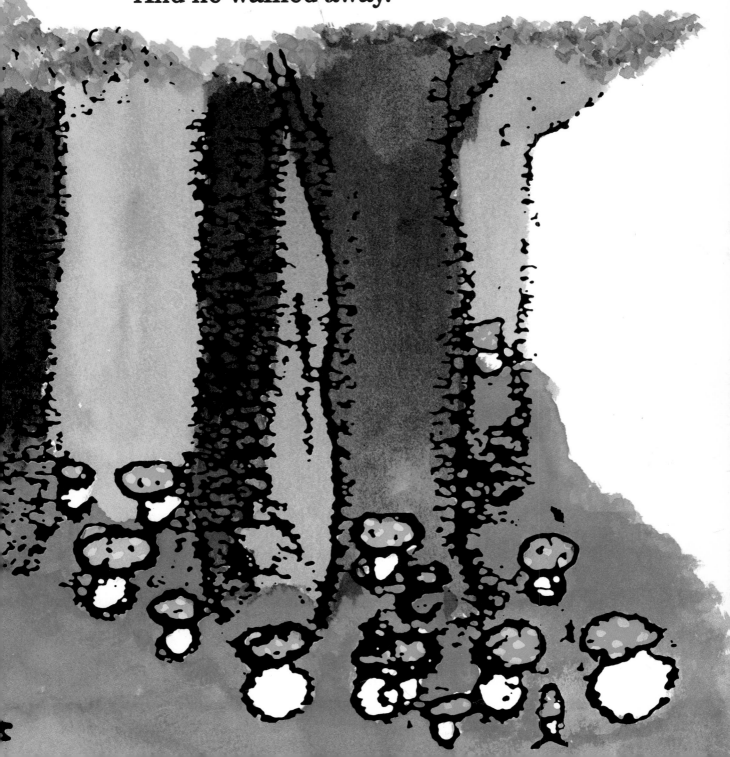

The next day the ogre heard some birds
singing and laughing outside his house.
They were practicing a song the frog
had taught them:

"Not seeing past his pointy nose,
The ogre looked into my eyes.
He ran to hide because he thought
That I was twice his size."

The ogre was furious. "That frog king tricked me!" he shouted. "I will eat that frog! I will eat them all!"
But when he ran outside, there wasn't an animal in sight.
The ogre went back into his house. "I should have caught that frog and fried him for lunch," he thought. "I should have grabbed those birds and chopped them up for dessert. But it's too late now. Soon the whole forest will know what a fool I was."

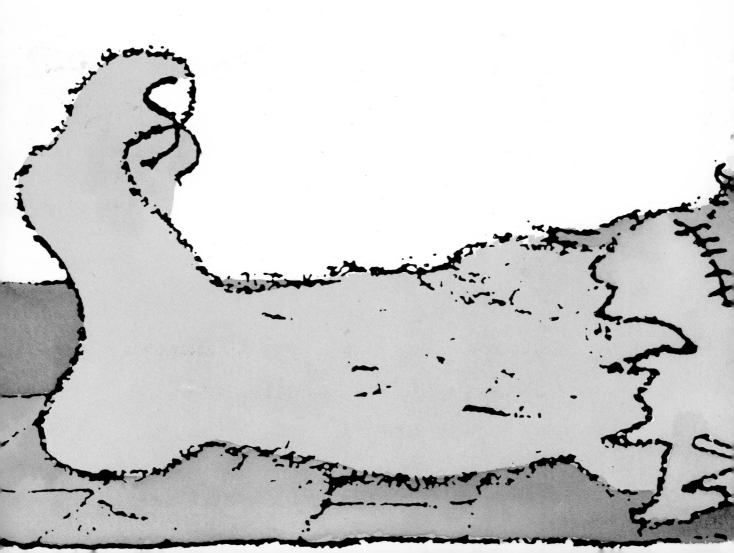

The ogre was so ashamed that

he left the forest forever.

"Hurrah for the frog king!"
all the animals cried.
"We're safe at last."
And the frog and
the field mouse
danced for joy.

Library of Congress Cataloging-in-Publication Data

Solotareff, Grégoire.
The ogre and the frog king.
Translation of: Monsieur l'Ogre et la rainette.
Summary: A frog tricks a giant ogre into believing
the frog is the bigger and more powerful of the two,
so that the ogre will stop eating the forest animals.
[1. Frogs—Fiction.   2. Animals—Fiction.
3. Monsters—Fiction]   I. Title.
PZ7.S69620g   1988   [E]   87-8531
ISBN 0-688-07078-7
ISBN 0-688-07079-5 (lib. bdg.)

Copyright © 1986 by L'Ecole des Loisirs   Translation copyright © 1988 by William Morrow & Co., Inc.
First published in France by L'Ecole des Loisirs under the title *Monsieur L'Ogre et La Rainette*